The Fall of Heaven

Kyuka Lilymjok

ISBN 978-978-969-224-8

Published by:
Free Pen Publishers
10 Lachlan Close, Maitama, Abuja

Any people depicted in stock imagery provided by Thinkstock are models, and such images are being used for such purposes only.

This book is printed on acid-free paper.

The views expressed in this work are solely those of the author and do not necessarily reflect the views of the publisher. The publisher hereby disclaims any responsibility for them.

To my wife Maria and my children: Justice, Sunfair
and Fairprincess

While common sense is
Always out of fuel
There is always fuel
In the tank of stupidity

Prologue

A great sight appeared in heaven: a woman
clothed with the sun, with the moon under her feet
and a crown of twelve stars on her head. She was
pregnant and cried out in pain as she was about to
give birth. Then another sight appeared in heaven:
an enormous red dragon with seven heads and ten
horns and seven crowns on its heads. Its tail swept
a third of the stars out of the sky and flung them to
the earth. The dragon stood in front of the woman
who was about to give birth, so that it might
devour her child the moment he was born. She
gave birth to a son ... who "will rule all the nations
with an iron scepter. And her child was snatched
up to God and to his throne. The woman fled into
the wilderness to a place prepared for her by God,
where she might be taken care of for 1,260 days.

Then war broke out in heaven. Michael and his
angels fought against the dragon, and the dragon
and his angels fought back. But he was not strong
enough, and they lost their place in heaven. The
great dragon was hurled down—that ancient
serpent called the devil, or Satan, who leads the
whole world astray. He was hurled to the earth,
and his angels with him.

When the dragon saw that he had been hurled
to the earth, he pursued the woman who had given
birth to the male child. The woman was given the
two wings of a great eagle, so that she might fly to
the place prepared for her in the wilderness, where

she would be taken care of for a time ... out of the serpent's reach. Then from his mouth the serpent spewed water like a river to overtake the woman and sweep her away with the torrent. But the earth helped the woman by opening its mouth and swallowing the river that the dragon had spewed out of his mouth. Then the dragon was enraged at the woman and went off to wage war against the rest of her offspring—those who keep God's commands and hold fast their testimony about Jesus.

Chapter One

For weeks, Sabi has been bedridden with a strange sickness people rumoured was caused by the sick man's drinking habit. He was a chronic drunk to whom liquor had become water. For weeks, the sick man could neither eat nor get off the bed to ease himself. An old man in his village said he had so emaciated that his ribs could be counted much easier than his teeth. Both the sick man and his relations expected death long ago, but death delayed its arrival for strange reasons like the strange sickness. He was indeed the creaking door that hung longest; the fish bone in the throat that would not go down and would not come out.

When impatience was turning to exasperation, death finally arrived to relieve both patient and his relations. In the words of the old man yet, were death something people could see, both the sick man and his relations would have given it the treatment given to a delinquent child: a rap on the head with a fist as a rebuke for coming so late.

The pastor who preached at Sabi's funeral was careful not to say Sabi will make heaven as pastors are wont to during funeral ceremonies. This was usually done to console relations of the deceased. Sabi was a drunk who never forgot to drink on any day. Whether the pastor avoided saying he will make heaven because he had received communication from heaven on the matter or because he was part of the common belief in the village that if there is hell, Sabi will not miss it, was not clear which was the case.

A young man at the funeral asked his friend how he thinks Sabi would turn up in the hereafter.

'With empty bottles and kegs of palm wine of course,' the friend said, laughing.

The young man who asked the question also laughed. 'Unless he develops more hands and heads in the hereafter, he would need angels to help him carry the empty bottles and kegs of palm wine he would appear there with,' he said without let in his laughter.

'Why should angels help one going to hell carry his things?' the second young man queried. 'That is the work of demons. Demons that drank with him on earth would be on hand to carry his bottles and kegs of palm wine as he staggered towards hell. How do you expect God would allow angels soil their holiness with beer bottles and kegs of palm wine?'

'Well, you see angels would be needed to testify against him before God,' said the first young man. 'So, I think they would carry the bottles, not demons. Demons cannot be trusted not to be up to tricks and deviousness in a matter like this.'

'You may have a point there,' said the second young man. 'But you see when it comes to happenings in hell, only the devil can give evidence. So demons who live in the hell of the earth as that of the sky are better placed to testify against Sabi than angels who do not.'

'I can see your point,' said the first young man.

'Perhaps you have not heard the story that made me say what I just said,' the second young man said with a mischievous gleam on his face.

'Which story is that?' the first young man asked, excitedly. His friend was a story merchant and each story he told never failed to excite his audience.

'In an armed-robbery trial, all the four witnesses called by the defence were convicted armed robbers,' the second young man began. 'The most innocent of these witnesses was the one that had suffered three convictions. Seeing the quality of the defence witnesses, the prosecution lawyer urged the court not to place any weight on their evidence because according to him they were men of inglorious character. To this submission, the lawyer for the defence fired back that when it comes to happenings in hell, only the devil can give evidence. In an armed robbery trial, it is not pastors or imams that are qualified to give evidence, but armed robbers.'

The first young man roared with laughter. 'I think something is fundamentally wrong with lawyers,' he said when he stopped laughing. 'They are way, way far from heaven into hell.'

'You can say that again and even the tortoise will not disagree with you,' said the second young man. 'My lawyer friend also told me how in another armed robbery case, lawyers for the accused by various defences were able to free him from the charge. When the jury came out and declared: 'Not Guilty;' O'Really the acquitted accused involuntarily exclaimed: 'Wonderful! Does that mean I can spend the money?'

The first young man swayed from side to side with laughter. 'If the jury could not convict O'Really, O'Really not only convicted the jurors but sentenced them to eternal shame,' he said when he got back his breath. 'With all these bad traits, how can lawyers make heaven?'

'They said about 400 years ago, one lawyer was able to make heaven. Since then, none has attained that feat again,' said the second young man.

Again, the first young man laughed most heartily

'Do you know what my lawyer friend further told me?' the second young man asked in a buoyant tone.

'No,' the second young man said wondering what was coming next.

'He said law is the only profession that would be needed either in heaven or hell. Neither Engineering nor pharmacy would be needed because both God and the devil have done all the engineering and provide all the drugs needed in heaven and hell.'

Again, the first young man laughed. 'I suspect the devil to have come up with the idea of the law profession in the first place and I suspect he is the life grand patron of it,' he said still laughing.

Perhaps because as it is on earth, it is in heaven, Sabi did not make heaven, but made hell. Such was the love of the devil for him that he himself was at the gate of hell to welcome home *a beloved son in whom he is well pleased*.

Chapter Two

Shortly after Sabi's death, Bilba his father heartbroken by his death also died. Despite his numerous faults, Sabi's father loved his son deeply. Though delinquent and wayward, Sabi was the apple of his father's eyes if he was the eyesore of God's eyes. With many faults, someone said Sabi's father loved him to a fault. It was therefore not surprising the father could not survive the death of the son for long.

Unlike his son, Bilba was a religious man who delighted in living a righteous life. While both father and son were alive, people kept saying the porcupine has given birth to a wall gecko.

As Sabi was expected by everyone who knew him and his life style to make hell, everyone who knew Bilba his father believed he would make heaven. Perhaps because as it is on earth, it is in heaven, Bilba made heaven. Such was the pleasure of heaven with him that an archangel was at the gate of heaven to welcome home *a beloved son in whom God,* popularly called His Peace in heaven, *is well pleased.*

Conditions for making heaven kept changing from time to time. One time it could be industry and firmness, not even holiness. Another time it could be fairness and courage, not even righteousness. At the time Sabi died, three things were needed for a dead person to be admitted into heaven. First, the dead person while on earth must have had a good heart whether he believed in God or not. Secondly, he must have been an ingenious person capable of resolving complex issues. Thirdly, he must not have been prone to idle talk.

The gate of heaven was not made of metal or any of the stuff gates on earth are made of. It was made of a thorny tree called the heavenway tree. The heavenway tree spanned to shut people out of heaven and shrank to let people into heaven. Before shutting a person out of heaven or letting him in, the tree ascertained whether or not the person had met the three requirements for admission into heaven. It ascertained by spanning like a bed for a dead person to lie on it. If he lay on it and was not pricked by its thorns, he was a person fit for heaven and was let in. If he was pricked by the thorns, he was unworthy of heaven and was shut out.

Before admitting anyone into heaven, the heavenway tree embraced the person who had made heaven in what was called embrace for heaven worthiness before releasing him into heaven. Once embraced by the heavenway tree, a person who had made heaven could not think well or remember much who he was.

Before Bilba died and went to heaven, heaven was a Garden of Eden in a literal as in a metaphorical sense. In a metaphorical sense, heaven was a place of rustic innocence. Heaveners did no evil and heard no evil. Like trees, heaveners could not irritate anyone nor could they be irritated. They were like Adam and Eve before they ate the forbidden fruits. In a literal sense, heaven was a Garden of Eden because the tree of the knowledge of good and evil in the Garden of Eden was in heaven.

Unknown to those who made heaven and even angels, the tree of the knowledge of good and evil was among the trees in the wilderness of heaven. East of heaven, there was a wilderness angels and heaveners seeking solitude from the halleluiah and praise-the-lord noise of heaven often repaired to for quiet and peace. While heaveners looking for excitement went to gaze at the ripples of the well of wonders, heaveners after solitude went to the wilderness. The wilderness full of trees and tall grasses stretched to the end of one's vision. Cascading through the wilderness were rivers and streams. Dotting it were water springs, waterfalls, hills and mountains.

The only being beside God who knew the tree of the knowledge of good and evil was in the wilderness of heaven was John the Baptist. Not even Jesus, Peter or Paul knew the tree was there. John the Baptist knew the tree was there because as on earth, he lived in the wilderness in heaven. Living in the wilderness, he knew every tree and what type of tree it was.

Since his arrival in heaven and knowing of the wilderness, hardly a day passed without Bilba going to the wilderness for quiet and peace. For Bilba, the wilderness was the real heaven not where His Peace was with all the noise of worshipping him.

Whenever he was in the wilderness, he thought in a fitful way about John the Baptist and his sermons in the wilderness of the earth. As a Christian, John the Baptist had always intrigued and fascinated him than any other prophet; than even Jesus Christ himself. A man who took to the wilderness living on locusts and honey so that he could serve His Peace and hear from him away from the noise and distraction of the town was surely no ordinary man. Wearing leaves and skins of animals, he was a widow in dust and ashes all his life; a man that calibrated and widowed himself to serve His Peace. There is no proof he married or had children. When Jesus said among men born of women, none is greater than John the Baptist, Bilba thought he should have said among men born of women none is as great as John the Baptist and this includes me. If John the Baptist had the humility of saying Jesus was greater than him and that he could not even carry Jesus' shoes, Jesus should have shown similar humility by saying he was unworthy to be compared with John the Baptist. Jesus only fasted forty days and forty nights. John the Baptist fasted in the wilderness all his life. Jesus was crucified; John the Baptist was beheaded.

In heaven with a fractioned mind, Bilba could not think well of anything or remember much of anything. In the wilderness of heaven, all he did was to sit down or wander the wilderness enjoying the breeze that always blew through it in the morning and evening. One evening while sitting in the wilderness, John the Baptist appeared to him in animal skins and leaves. On earth, he had images of John the Baptist in his mind. In heaven with only part of his mind, seeing John the Baptist he could not immediately recognize him. But John the Baptist immediately recognized him. His thoughts and love of John the Baptist while on earth communicated themselves to the forerunner of Christ also making him like him. It was because the forerunner of Christ liked him that he appeared to him to reveal one of the secrets of heaven to him.

The secret of heaven John the Baptist revealed to Bilba was the presence of the tree of the knowledge of good and evil in the wilderness of heaven and what it does to a heavener when he embraced it. The way John the Baptist discovered the tree of the knowledge of good and evil was the way he led Bilba to discover it.

Wandering the wilderness one evening, John the Baptist, without knowing the deeper character of the tree, embraced the tree of the knowledge of good and evil as he was wont to. For quite a while he stood with his hands wrapped round the tree while he swayed about. As he stood with his hands about the trunk of the tree, an electric sensation went through him. His body sagged, his eyes rolled out and he fell down on his back unconscious. When he came to, he could think and remember who he was. He could also recall this was the tree of the knowledge of good and evil he knew in the wilderness of the earth. Sitting by the tree thinking, he could recall when he lost much of his mind. When he died and came to the gate of heaven, he had all his mind with him. It was when the heavenway tree embraced him to let him into heaven that he became more of vegetation than man. Thinking of the situation, he felt duped and angry. Since then he had thought of hitting back but never came round to doing so until he saw Bilba a man he knew loved him so dearly and a man he also loved dearly. This man was wandering the wilderness of heaven with little mind and quite unhappy. He decided to give him back his full mind by leading him to the tree of the knowledge of good and evil and making him embrace it the way he did years back. This he thought would make both he and Bilba happier, if God would be unhappier.

Chapter Three

What John the Baptist experienced when he embraced the tree of the knowledge of good and evil was what Bilba experienced when he embraced it.

'This is the tree of the knowledge of good and evil whose fruits Adam and Eve ate,' John the Baptist said after Bilba had embraced the tree.

'Who are you?' Bilba asked.

'I am John the Baptist.'

'I thought so,' Bilba said, excitedly. 'So, this is the tree of the knowledge of good and evil that made Adam and Eve to sin?'

'Yes, this is the tree that brought sin and death to the world. In heaven, it is the same tree you embrace to recover your mind. Before you embraced this tree, you were more of a walking and talking vegetation than human.'

For a while Bilba did not say anything. He was thinking. He was once more a being that could think. Thinking, he could recollect when he lost much of his mind. It was when the heavenway tree embraced him.

'Why should God be interested in taking away the minds of people?' he asked feeling despondent.

'You will soon find out,' John the Baptist said.

The first night Bilba spent in heaven after embracing the tree of the knowledge of good and evil, he could not sleep. All he could hear were the cries of pain of his son Sabi. Sabi's screams of pain pierced through his heart like a thousand pins leaving him perhaps in more pain than his son.

On this night, Sabi was not calling his name in his cries of pain. Though his son was not calling him, he could distinctively recognize the agony of his son from the agonies of other inmates of the nether region. That his son was not calling him for help did not significantly lessen his pain. The following day Sabi started screaming and calling on him to come and bail him from this place of torment.

Before his death, Bilba had thought of heaven as a place of pure bliss and leisure. Though he had read the story of Lazarus and the rich iniquitous man, at no time did it cross his mind he would be Lazarus in heaven and his son the rich iniquitous man in hell. The moment his son started screaming calling on him to come and rescue him, Bilba to the shock of many angels and His Peace also started screaming to be allowed to go and rescue his son or he would leave heaven to live in hell with his son.

Everyone in heaven was taken aback by Bilba 's screams. What was the matter with him? many heaveners wondered. Was he insane?

His Peace was also wondering: Has the fellow embraced the tree of the knowledge of good and evil? Who could have revealed this secret to him so soon after his coming to heaven?

As fellow heaveners were wondering if he was insane, Bilba was wondering what the matter was with them hearing the cries of their loved ones for help and not being moved to agony by such cries. Then he remembered they were with little mind and little memory. Immediately he resolved to give them full mind and memory by taking them to the tree of the knowledge of good and evil to be given full mind and memory.

Within two weeks of acquiring full mind and memory, Bilba took virtually all heaveners to the tree of the knowledge of good and evil to embrace it and recover their full minds and memories. After many heaveners acquired full minds and memories, there was palpable disquiet in heaven. When Bilba screamed and leapt up to go to hell to rescue his son, other heaveners also started screaming and leaping towards hell to do likewise to their relations there.

For a while, heaven was full of commotion as much as hell was. Heaveners were leaping into the air screaming to be let out of heaven while angels were running around like beheaded chickens trying to quell the commotion and restrain the heaveners from streaming or flooding out of heaven. It was a grotesque and sorrowful sight His Peace and angels found unwholesome and distressing. What was going on they wondered in despair? What the hell was going on in heaven?

It was like the cacophony in heaven restored some peace in hell for the inmates of hades were no longer screaming like before. Heaveners clamouring for them to be freed from the torment of hell seemed to have given them hope that has quietened them. With less clamour for help from hell, there was less frenzy by heaveners to go to hell to help their relations. For a while, there was calm in heaven and hell albeit a pregnant one in both.

'I never thought or even suspected this is how heaven will be,' Bilba said to Yongwe who later became his best friend in heaven.

'Neither did I,' Yongwe said.

'Is this what you have been living with in heaven?' Bilba asked Yongwe who had been in heaven for a long time.

'This is how it has been my brother,' Yongwe said, sighing. 'Here people whistle past the graveyard while their hearts are either sinking or in their mouths. I made heaven but my daughter that made hell is no more in hell than I am.'

Here people whistle past the graveyard while their hearts are either sinking or in their mouths Bilba repeated what Yongwe had said smiling. 'It is cool hearing this popular American expression once more,' he said, his face brighter by a mile. 'By the way, I haven't seen any American since I arrived here. Do they have their own heaven here as they do on earth?'

'No,' Yongwe said, savouring a smile. 'You know America has both Paradise City and a town called Hell. Most Americans dying do not bother coming this way. They either head for their Paradise City on earth or their Hell there. Americans you know always have things their own way.'

Bilba chuckled. 'Back to what we were talking about,' he said; 'if things in heaven have been how they are now, why haven't you all defied His Peace and his angels and gone to hell to at least offer succour to your relations there if you can't rescue them?'

'You forget we did not have much mind?' Yongwe asked.

'I forgot,' Bilba said, scratching his head.

'Even with little minds, now and then some of us used to think of sneaking out of heaven to bail water from the well of wonders to quench the thirst of our relations in hell, but somehow never got round to doing so,' Yongwe said.

'Is there a well in this place?' Bilba asked with lively interest.

'Yes,' Yongwe replied. 'It is ripples from that well that cools the heat coming from hell so that it does not scorch us in heaven.

'From what I am seeing and hearing in this place, the last Lucifer is yet to arise,' Bilba said, pouting his lips petulantly.

Chapter Four

Between heaven and hell, there was a well popularly called the well of wonders from which ripples of water leapt into the air to absorb heat-waves from hell that are heaven-bound. Ripples from the well shot into the air almost a kilometre long and half a kilometre wide. Ripples from the well apart from being a shield around heaven from the heat of hell are one of the great wonders of heaven. The way the ripples fanned-out on coming out of the well while streaming upward is so magical that no science could explain it.

When ripples from the well of wonders captured heat-waves in the air, they redirected the captured heat-waves into the bowels of heaven only to spring out of the bowels of the well again into the air in all their beauty and majestic splendour. On earth, no water spring or waterfall came near the beauty and majesty of ripples from this well.

In the air, the ripples giggled and danced about as if drunk with excitement liberation from the enclosure of the well has given them. Viewing the sky through the ripples, the sky took a whitish hue that was enchanting in its beauty. About a kilometre away from the well, hell kept puffing heat-waves that looked like wriggling poles in the air.

There were many stories in heaven and hell about the well of wonders and the ripples rippling out of it. One story had it that the well was the bottomless pit His Peace threw the devil and the ripples coming out of the well were ripples generated by the devil in the water of the well. In addition to the ripples generated by his fall, the devil was also said to be using his tail to generate some of the ripples issuing out of the well. Not many heaveners or hellers credited these stories with belief because they failed to add up. How heavy was the devil and how big was the water of the well to generate such enormous ripples? Again, that the devil is about the earth doing mischief everywhere he goes means he had since swum out of the bottomless pit His Peace threw him. So how could he still be stirring ripples in a well he was out of?

Another story told about the well and the ripples welling out of it was that the well was connected with all the seas and oceans of heaven from which it drew water to spray the atmosphere in the form of the ripples. According to this story, the well was a sucking and vomiting pipe that sucked water from the seas and oceans of heaven, vomited it into the atmosphere only to suck it back and vomit it again into the seas and oceans.

Yet another story about the well and its ripples had it that the mighty hand of His Peace was in the waters of the well stirring them and pumping them up generating the ripples that spanned through the atmosphere. According to this story, His Peace who spat hell out of his mouth punched the water of the well into ripples to secure the chosen ones that made heaven.

Whichever story was true of the well of wonders and its ripples, the ripples of the well were a big attraction to denizens of heaven and would have even been a bigger attraction to inmates of hell had they liberty to leave hell and wander into the neighbourhood of hell the way heaveners had. Every day, heaveners bored by the routine of heaven wandered to the well to gaze at the ripples streaming out of the well. Though they gazed at the ripples every day and this had also become another routine, they never seemed bored by this routine. Each day, they gazed at the ripples from the well with about the same fascination they did the previous day. It was said the ripples carried a spell it cast on those viewing it.

Some days, heaveners got so engrossed with viewing the ripples of the well of wonders that they forgot or neglected their duties in heaven. Their main duty in heaven was to worship His Peace. This, they often found a boring routine. Finding the routine boring, they sometimes forgot or neglected to observe it when viewing the ripples. One day, a heavener captivated by the ripples was heard saying if His Peace was not careful, the well and its ripples may replace him as an object of worship.

'I agree with you,' said another heavener with him by the ripples. 'Why can't His Peace transform himself into the ripples of the well so that we can better worship him,' he went on in a trance-like state.

'You are certainly saying something there,' said the first heavener looking with amazement and excitement the fellow who just spoke. 'What a great idea you just expressed. If His Peace were to heed your suggestion, he would by so doing make heaven truly heavenly. Please someone should sound His Peace on this.'

A month after Bilba's death and arrival in heaven, there was another commotion in heaven because there was upheaval in hell. It now seemed to His Peace and his angels that since the arrival of Bilba, heaven has turned into a cave turmoil in hell echoed.

The disturbance in hell took place late in the evening when the sun was about to be swallowed by the distant horizon. Most heaveners were startled and rattled by the intensity of the commotion from hell. It was like the inmates of hell wanted to bring down hell the way Joshua and his army brought down the walls of Jericho. In a long, strident howl, they screamed and screeched as if molten iron bars were being driven through them.

Louder than other cries of agony heaveners had so far heard from hell since Bilba arrived, this cry of anguish was so banded together that it was impossible to separate the various cries that made it and allocate to individual hellers. So Bilba could not recognize in the cry the one that issued from his son. Because he could not recognize the cry of his son, he was not as moved to pity and heartbreak as when he heard the lone and plaintive cry of his son clamouring for help. If there was hell for His Peace in the loudness of the screams of the hellers, there was some salvation for him in that hell.

When the din of noise generated by the howling of the hell inmates died down, the lone and heart-wrenching cry of Sabi could be heard rising into the atmosphere and suffusing heaven with the pain and agony of the crier. 'Papa, papa, please help me. I am being roasted and melted in this place; please help me!'

Bilba was once more devastated. His heart was wrung from his chest by his son's plea for help and dashed on the floor of heaven. What sin did his son commit on earth to warrant the severe punishment he was now going through? he kept asking himself. Yes, his son was a drunk. Was this sin enough to subject him to this brutal and cruel punishment? By drinking he was not subjecting anyone to harm but himself. Even if he had killed someone, was such sin sufficient justification for the affliction he was going through and would go through forever? How was he as father to endure the cry of torment of his son through eternity? He had been in heaven only for weeks now. These weeks have been more hell than heaven. 'No, no, no!' he cried in agony. 'This is all very unfair. There is no scintilla or modicum of justice in all these. Your Peace, I can't endure the cry of pain from my son anymore! I must be allowed to go and rescue my son from hell or I will relocate there.'

For a while, His Peace did not say anything. He was thinking: this could not be ordinary. Someone must have revealed the most important secret of heaven to the heaveners. Who was it? Who knew the secret of embracing the tree of the knowledge of good and evil beside him? Who even knew the tree was in heaven? Even the Son and angels did not know these things. How could secrets he kept close to his chest for ages leaked out of him without his intelligence? What was he to do now that it seemed his most guarded secrets had been leaked? Was he to change his design of having hell next door to heaven? No, he would not do so. He would not allow common human beings he created to force his hands this way. What could they do beyond shouting, anyway? Nothing, as far as he could see and he could see very far. They would eventually have to accept and live with things the way they were. There was not going to be change in anything.

Not only was His Peace shocked by what Bilba said, he was shocked by his audacity in saying it. 'You are not the only one here with a son or relation in hell,' he said in a voice that carried part of his feelings.

'I know,' Bilba said. 'But we don't have the same heart. What the heart of one man can endure, that of another may not. What the heart of one man sees and laugh that of another man sees and cry.'

'Bilba is not alone in his anguish,' Yongwe said, feverishly. 'I have a daughter in hell. I can't endure her wailings there either. Her wailings are tearing my heart apart.'

'It is the same with me,' said another heavener. 'I have a nephew in hell. His lamentations are making me freak out.'

His Peace signalled an angel to approach him. For a while he and the angel conferred in undertones. When they were through, the angel went back to where he was before His Peace motioned him.

'I have heard your different complaints and entreaties on the fate of your relations in hell,' His Peace began speaking. 'Unfortunately, nothing can be done about their situation. Heaven and hell were designed by me this way to make hellers see what their sins have denied them and heaveners to see what their virtues have secured them from. There is nothing I can do about it.'

'So, neither hell nor heaven can be taken faraway from each other so that I no longer hear the torturing cry of my niece?' a man asked in agony.

'That can't be done,' His Peace said. 'Heaven and hell where designed to be next door.'

'You are His Peace – a Supreme Being of possibilities. I thought with you nothing is impossible,' said a heavener.

'Not only is he a Supreme Being of possibilities but a merciful Being of sympathy,' said another heavener. 'Please, Your Peace have mercy.'

'No doubt I am His Peace of possibilities,' His Peace said, tartly. 'But I am also His Peace of impossibilities where divine designs are concerned. Yes, I am merciful, but I am also merciless where sin is concerned.'

"It is bad engineering, poor town planning to have hell next door to heaven,' a heavener grumbled. 'The engineers and town planners should be called back to site.'

'Heaven was lost when His Peace decided to have it in the neighbourhood of hell,' another heavener murmured. 'The gates of heaven shouldn't open to the gates of hell.'

'On earth, prison – the hell of the convicted criminals, is an outskirts affair; it is not so mixed up with residential houses,' said yet another heavener.

His Peace did not say anything. It seemed he did not hear the murmurings of the heaveners for he was again conferring with an angel.

Chapter Six

Though a drunk, Sabi was a kind hearted person who was always ready to assist people who needed help. Returning home drunk from Madam See-Well beer parlour one evening, he came by an old woman and two little children who looked like they had not eaten for days.

The woman was aged and looked like life had been hard on her, not only lately, but most, if not all of her being. She was emaciated and crooked from abdomen to head. From all indications the children with her were her grandchildren. It had become very common for young girls to conceive out of wedlock and abandon the children with their old parents if they did not abandon them in the bush. The children with the old woman looked to Sabi like children abandoned by their mother with their grandmother.

Though within the town, where the old woman and the children were there were no houses. The place was a bush with tall grasses and shrubs scattered here and there. Because of where they were, when Sabi first sighted them, he wondered in his drunkenness if they were spirits. As he drew nearer them however, he felt they were humans.

The old woman was sitting under a tree by the roadside when Sabi came along staggering and mumbling incoherent words. In his armpit was a bottle of beer he bought at Madam See-Well; in his hand was a small keg of palm wine he was drinking as he staggered home.

At the beer parlour, he kept reaching for Madam See-Well's behind whenever she moved near him to serve him beer or other customers. Each time he reached out for her backside, she would brush aside his groping hands or swerve from their reach. The last time he reached for her behind before leaving the beer parlour and she skirted away, he said, 'Madam See-Well; I am seeing well but you don't want to give me what I am seeing. Madam See Well, though you can see well, I don't think you can see what I am seeing behind you. What I am seeing behind and in front of you are taking you to hell, not to heaven. Madam See-Well, though you can see well, you can't see this one because it is behind you. You see Madam See-Well, it is women selling beer and women selling their bodies that will escort men to hell. But you don't need to blame yourself too much for this. It is not just now this thing started. It started in the Garden of Eden. It was Eve that escorted Adam out of the Garden of Eden to hell. You don't need to feel too guilty Madam See-Well. The path you are treading was trod thousands of years by your ancestress. Heaven …? I thought heaven ended in the Garden of Eden and all we have left is hell.'

Before leaving the beer parlour, he always bought a keg of palm wine and a bottle of beer he said would escort him home. The liquor in his stomach or as he always put it, the petrol in his tank would not take him home. He needed petrol in two jerry cans to make it home. On the way, when he started feeling sober, he would gulp more palm wine or beer for him to continue to float along the road. As he lurched forward and backward bombed and tanked up, the keg of palm wine in his hand and bottle of beer in his armpit swished about, surprisingly neither the palm wine in the keg nor the beer in the bottle spilling much on the road. They only spilled in his stomach. The little of them that spilled on the road, he said spilled into the mouths of his ancestors to cheer them in the land of the dead.

When he came by the old woman and the two children, he immediately became sober. That was something with him. He always became sober immediately he came by misery. Those who knew this aspect of him said he became a drunk to drown the misery of life not knowing that misery is a good swimmer.

Now by the poor old woman and her children, Sabi was sober and very sad. While the old woman sat forlornly by, the two children less aware of the terror of poverty and their unfortunate circumstances were running about playing. Around them darkness was closing in.

Because he was always about, Sabi knew many people in Bojua and many people knew him. Being about apart, Bojua was not a very big town. It was a small-town people easily got to know each other. Sabi was surprised he did not know the old woman by the roadside. However, that he did not know her made no difference to his pity for her and her children. Night was crawling forward, but the old woman was still outside with her children perhaps hoping to get what to eat that night. He fumbled his pockets for money to give them. He found a hundred sicom note and gave the old woman who curtsied while receiving it. It was the biggest amount of money anyone had given her in days.

It was a blowy day trees and grasses danced to the drums of the wind and the agama lizard nods its head in celebration of the favours of the day. When Sabi gave the old woman the money, a gentle breeze swept through the about bush and the grasses around the old woman swayed as if thanking Sabi for what he had done. Behind the old woman, an agama lizard on a little anthill in the bush nodded its head as if approving Sabi's benevolence. Not far off the agama lizard, butterflies in a little swarm were flitting in the air and the bush as if in a party that has gone heady; as if drunk with the generosity of a drunk.

The hundred sicom Sabi gave the old woman was the only money he had. Yet he was very happy giving her the money. The smile on her wizened face when he gave her the money flooded his heart with happiness. The smile dissolved the wrinkles on her face and she looked a lot younger. As the smile dissolved her wrinkles, it seemed to have withered twenty years of her age.

But Sabi was soon sad again. The old woman had curtsied while receiving the money from him. Why should a woman old enough to be his mother curtsy to collect money from him? Tears were now shining in his eyes. Cursing the government for not providing for the poor and needy, he hurriedly walked away from the old woman and her children before the tears rolled on his cheeks. Stoned and stewed once more, he staggered on towards his house, three sheets to the wind and eight feathers to the air.

Shortly after Sabi left, the pastor of a local church dressed in his cassock appeared, moving in the direction Sabi moved a while ago. He was on his way to the church for evening service. With piety on his face, he was in cheerful thoughts. Last Sunday offering was good. It was more like a bumper harvest than an offering. It looked like the flock was leaving Ananias and Sapphira alone in their miserliness and was moving in the direction of the widow and her mite. It looked like it was moving from Cain in his farmlands to Abel in his pastures. How he prayed it remains in the generous purse of the widow and the open-handed pastures of Abel.

The old woman on seeing the pastor was full of hope. She waved at him making a begging sign. But the pastor appearing not to have seen her, swept past her and her children in his haste to get to church to serve God.

Unknown to the old woman, Sabi and the pastor, two youngsters sitting on the window of a nearby uncompleted building smoking weeds saw when Sabi gave the old woman money and walked past, and when the pastor gave her nothing and walked past. As soon as the pastor walked past, they began talking about what they saw.

'The pastor has turned out the fig tree the old woman went to for fruits only to find there were no fruits on it,' one of the youngsters said in a mirthful tone. 'Like Jesus, the old woman should have cursed him.'

'And the drunk has turned out the rock that gave water to the old woman without Moses even striking it,' said the other youngster.

'The Priest and the Levite left the man who had fallen among thieves to death while the Good

Samaritan rescued him from death,' said the first youngster.

'A pastor who expects offerings in the church is too miserly to make offerings on the street,' said the second youngster.

'A drunk who receives no offering in the church is the one making offerings on the street,' said the first youngster.

'The times are strange.'

'They are indeed strange.'

'We have come to a time trees are not producing fruits while rocks are producing water. The times are indeed strange.'

'This pastor lacking gold and silver, if indeed he lacks the precious metals, also seems to lack heart.'

'The times are not only strange, they are evil.'

As Sabi cared about people he did not know, he cared even more for his parents. When either his mother or father was unhappy because of one problem or the other, Sabi was sad and ready to help out.

Chapter Seven

For days, Bilba sulked in heaven following His Peace's decision to stick to his original divine order of keeping sinners forever in hell. Also sulking with Bilba were other denizens of heaven with relations in hell. Angels spoke to them but they rarely spoke back. When they did, they barked at the angels like famished dogs. Instead of speaking to angels, they showed more inclination to talk to demons when they could find them. They felt the latter could make things less hard for their relations in hell. Heaven, meant to be a home of peace and happiness, was seething and festering with resentment and hate among those who made it.

'This place will implode sooner than later,' Bilba kept saying to himself. 'I can't be sitting here smiling at His Peace, clapping for him or waving my hands in adoration of him while my son is wailing and gnashing his teeth in hell in a so-called second death. No, it will not work.'

As he sat in the wilderness of heaven one day thinking of how he would rescue his son Sabi from hell, he overheard two angels talking animatedly to each other. Angels not only had different appearances from other denizens of heaven, they had different voices. Their voices were booming and piercing.

'The idea of having hell next door to heaven is turning out not a very hot one,' Bilba heard one angel saying to the other.

'If it is not a hot idea near hell, is it far from hell it will be?' the other angel said and laughed.

'Be serious for once,' the first angel said also laughing.

'You are right,' said the second angel. 'His Peace's original plan of having hell next door to heaven so that those who make heaven will appreciate it more seeing and hearing the torment in hell and those who make hell will see and hear the merriment in heaven is backfiring.'

'From day one, I never thought it would work,' said the first angel.

'If you thought it will not work, why didn't you say so to His Peace when he was incubating the plan?' said the second angel.

'As if you don't know the imperial one,' said the first angel. 'How do you expect him to take counsel from a common angel?'

'His Peace seems guilty of what he accused, convicted and sentenced the devil for: pride'

'Ssh ...,someone may be passing by. Fields have eyes and forests have ears.'

'Is another pride before a fall on the way?'

'Ssh ...'

'That Bilba man looks like trouble to me,' the second angel said, changing topic. 'I think admitting him into heaven is another mistake of His Peace.'

Bilba listening to the two angels caught his breath.

'I also think so,' said the first angel. 'But I don't think he would be alone in causing the trouble you fear he might. Other heaveners would join him in the trouble he may cause.'

'Thinking of the situation now,' said the second angel, 'I am rather surprised it took this long for those who make heaven to agitate for the release of their relations in hell.'

'I am as surprised as you are,' said the first angel, standing up where he had been sitting. 'There must be something going on in heaven now that we don't know. A cricket is chirring, but we don't know what it is chirring about. The owl is hooting a coming evil we know nothing of. Let's move around instead of sitting in one place talking all day.' Saying this, the first angel began walking in the opposite direction of where Bilba was. The second angel followed him.

Bilba sat down where he had been standing and listening to the two angels. This was something he thought. The way angels kotow and grovel before His Peace, he never thought they were capable of talking the way they just spoke. Before His Peace, all one heard was halleluiah and praise the lord to all His Peace did or said. He was an all-correct His Peace. If the angels were surprised that before now there had been no agitation in heaven by heaveners with relations in hell, he was much more surprised by the way they spoke behind His Peace. What all these goes to show is that as it is on earth, it is in heaven. Angels before His Peace in heaven were as full of pretence and hypocrisy as courtiers before the king on earth were full of pretence and hypocrisy. Politics was everywhere and truth was falling through the cracks. There was hope of success for the insurrection he was thinking of if he could play the politics of heaven well. It seemed there were

many falling angels that would be ready to rise up
against His Peace with him.

Chapter Eight

Before his death, Sabi, one rainy season, had ridden his bicycle to another village to drink. While in the village, rain fell. When the rain finished falling, Sabi set out on his bicycle to return home. As he rode the bicycle, hunger began to bite him. Apart from the beer he drank, he had eaten nothing that day. In the pangs of hunger, he remembered beancake he bought and tied on the carrier of his bicycle. He alighted from the bicycle and untied the beancake from the carrier. Sitting on the bicycle with one leg on the ground, he began eating the beancake. When he picked the last beancake and bit it, a little boy ran along the path he was. He gave the half-eaten beancake in his hand to the little boy who eagerly collected it. He came down from the bicycle and washed his hands in the water of a furrow, then rode away on his bicycle.

Konsa the boy Sabi gave the half-eaten beancake to never forgot this act of kindness. Like Sabi, he had not eaten anything that day. However, unlike Sabi who did not eat because he was more preoccupied with drinking liquor, Konsa did not eat because there was nothing for him to eat. When he collected the beancake from Sabi and began eating it, he stood by watching Sabi washing his hands in the water of the furrow. He watched him climb his bicycle and watched him ride away until he disappeared in the distance.

Konsa never forgot Sabi's act of kindness. The image of Sabi washing his hands in the water of the furrow after giving him the half-eaten beancake was permanently etched in his mind. Images of things that later happened to him in life faded away, but this image remained. All his life, he lived in the hope that one day he would do something good to Sabi in appreciation of his kindness, but never got round to doing so to the time Sabi died.

A couple of weeks after Bilba 's death, Konsa died in a cave exploration he undertook with his friends. Unlike Sabi however, Konsa made heaven. In heaven he could hear Sabi crying for a morsel of water to be dropped on his parched tongue and throat and he could remember vividly how so many years on earth Sabi had placed a morsel of beancake on his tongue when he was most famished and he felt really bad. Like Sabi's father, he wanted to help Sabi, but His Peace would not allow him.

'Your son was a good man on earth; I wonder why he is in hell,' Konsa said to Bilba.

'You knew him on earth?' Bilba asked surprised and excited.

'I did,' Konsa said. 'I knew him on earth as a good man. I am surprised he is in hell.'

'His Peace said he is in hell because he was a drunk on earth,' Bilba said.

'I don't share His Peace's resentments on this,' Konsa said. 'He was a drunk, who did he hurt by his drunkenness?'

'You ask me.'

'Yes, I ask you and wonder at the same time.'

'As far as I know, the only person he hurt was himself.'

'So he is burning in hell for hurting himself?'

'That's how it is.'

'This is absurd.'

'With His Peace, absurd things are what you see every day,' Bilba said. 'With him, Sabi's body was not his property but His Peace's temple.

Drinking alcohol, he said Sabi desecrated his temple.'

'Perhaps Sabi desecrated his temple; but he is burning down his temple. He is not making sense to me,' Konsa said.

'Ssh...'

'Honestly, I don't see any sense in this.'

'I think His Peace's reasoning is that the temple has been so desecrated he can no longer live in it. So, he decided to burn it down.'

Perhaps to relieve themselves of the anguish they were both in, the two men began speaking in a hubbub on issues that bore little connection with their anguish:

'If he can't live in it, can't the devil and his demons?'

'Well, perhaps that is why he is in hell where the devil and his demons are. But the devil and his demons are not meant to live in human bodies but in pigs.'

'Fortunately for them, pigs are never in short supply. They will never want for houses.'

'Fortunately for pigs, they are vaccinated by the devil and his demons against all evil and therefore fear no evil. So good are the affairs of the world for pigs that a pig in shit is a happy pig.'

'Some of the unfortunate behaviour you see in the devil are from pigs and some of the dirty behaviour you see in pigs are from the devil.'

'Pigs are physical wandering demons on earth or at least wandering houses for demons. The snorting sound coming from pigs are demons groaning inside their sty. Wandering pigs are wandering demons.'

'Wherever you see pigs, demons are not far off; dirty and wayward behaviours like drunkenness is also not far off.'

'You look so young; how did you die?'

'By the hands of misadventure. I and some friends went on cave exploration only for one of the caves we were exploring to collapse on us. None of us survived.'

'Cave exploration? Ah ... The cave is a grave. Exploring caves is exploring graves. Exploring graves is like invoking death on oneself. Whoever does so shouldn't be surprised if he does not come out alive from the cave he is exploring.'

Talking about graves, reminds me of the dust in Buadom where I came from. So much dust in that place that one was literally walking in a grave of dust. Already walking inside dust, the wind would just pack dust and dump on you. Every time you are walking on the road, you are literally walking in a grave of dust from which you keep rising when the same wind clears some of it.

'Buadom is Africa,' Bilba said, his voice sounding far and distant. 'Most of Africa is like Buadom, a hot sun and plenty dust.'

'Elsewhere people are walking under a cool sun and inside mist – a grave of water. In a grave of water, in a bathtub full of water and soap, they are washed all the time and therefore have fresh and becoming skins,' Konsa went on speaking more to himself than to Bilba. 'In Buadom, people are walking under a hot sun and dust and are looking like charred effigies from the place over there; like wrestlers in a dust bowl.'

At this point, a bell rang and a drum sounded. It was time for songs and drums in praise of His Peace.

'How can I dance to these drums while my son is wailing in fire?' Bilba wondered to himself.

'Doing so is unnatural to me,' Konsa said. 'It is not just a case of Nero fiddling while Rome burned or chasing rats while one's house is on fire; it is a case of laughing while sitting on thorns.'

'The fire burning my son has melted my legs and hands,' Bilba said. 'I am without legs and hands to dance and clap.'

'We must find a way of rescuing your son from that place,' Konsa said gruffly.

'If it requires befriending the devil to do so, I will befriend him,' Bilba swore, panting with emotion.

Chapter Nine

A month after Sabi's death, Loco his friend was at Madam See-Well beer parlour as usual. There were so many drunks at the beer parlour that they spilled out into the street. Even without so many people in the beer parlour, some drunks always preferred sitting outside where they would enjoy fresh air and a commanding view of the surroundings. Now with many people in the parlour, those outside sprawled out like worshippers in an open-air mass. As they drank, bawdy Jokes and ribaldry flowed to and fro alongside the beer that flowed to and fro.

Loco was Sabi's closest friend when the latter was alive. A tall lanky man, people said alcohol had eaten up Loco's insides. He used alcohol to rinse his mouth in the morning and drank it along with any food he was eating.

Loco loomed in his walk like one the ground was rejecting and was imposing himself on it. He kept blinking his eyes as if something had fallen into them and shaking his head as if mixing something inside it. People said he was blinking his eyes because he was seeing strange things and shaking his head so that the liquor he had taken would not float on his brain but would mix with it.

While walking, Loco kept waving his hand as if clearing something on his path. When Sabi died, many people thought he would stop drinking or at least reduce his liquor intake knowing it was liquor that killed his friend. But instead of Loco stopping or even reducing his liquor intake, he seemed to have increased it. When told God was sparing his life for him to repent, he said God was sparing his life because he had more days to drink.

'The antelope does not hear the music of its death and refuses to dance,' an elderly man said to his friend when Loco replied the way he did.

'Ajini, the evil one, is beating the sacred drum and Loco is dancing the dance of death,' the other elder said.

When Sabi died, people said Loco should have had a pastor for a friend. Instead, Loco girded his friendship with Paik a drunk without memory of when he started drinking and thought of when he would stop. Today Loco and Paik were at the beer parlour in the mammoth crowd sitting outside. The two drunks never sat inside the parlour. They always sat outside even when there was no one inside.

'Why should I sit inside that place?' Loco once asked Paik? 'Is it to see Madam See Well's behind which I can see more clearly here?'

'I wonder,' Paik said, taking a swig at the bottle of beer in front of him.

'Is it to hide myself so that people will not see me drinking?' Loco asked, again blinking his eyes.

'I wonder,' Paik said, belching.

'Whoever by my face and walk will not tell I am a drunk, let him come here and feed his eyes. I am a drunk who is yet to appoint the date he would stop drinking.'

'But Loco, drinking outside the way we do under the very eyes of heaven, isn't it too bad a thing to do?' Paik asked, grinning slyly.

'You may be right,' Loco said within hiccups. 'But I want heaven, as people, to bear me witness that I was not a hypocrite while on earth.'

'Talking about heaven, where do you think Sabi our friend is?' Paik asked drawing his lips to express satisfaction with the beer he was drinking.

'Hell of course!' Loco said, shaking his head. 'Apart from the fact that drunkenness is a sin that would make a drunk miss heaven, the path to heaven is a narrow path which a drunk in his drunkenness can easily miss. Narrow is the way and few are those on it; this is what the Bible says.'

Paik laughed.

'If on the wide paths of the world, drunks easily miss their way and enter the bush, what do you think would happen if a drunk finds himself on the narrow path of heaven?' Loco said, blinking his eyes rapidly.

Paik laughed.

'But the way to hell is a wide one if what the Bible says is anything to go by,' Loco went on when Paik stopped laughing. 'So, a drunk in his staggering, tottering and zigzagging movement can more easily follow the road to hell than the narrow path to heaven.'

'Loco, you are crazy,' Paik said.

'I agree,' Loco said, blinking rapidly. 'Too many forbidden fruits; too many apples for the devil to continue using to lead the world astray,' he went on after a momentary pause. 'Glittering cars, lewd women, trendy phones, magnificent houses are all alluring forbidden fruits the devil is using today to lead the world astray. Worse, it seems more forbidden fruits are sprouting out of the trees of the earth for the Wicked One to continue using to lure the sons and daughters of Eve to destruction.'

'Loco you are saying something weighty there,' Paik said in a surprisingly sober tone. 'I think you will not do badly as a pastor.'

'I hear you,' Loco hissed.

'Seriously, Loco, where do you think Sabi our friend is,' Paik drooled.

'You honestly want my mind on that?' Loco asked.

'Yes, though I know you have no mind,' Paik said, belching. 'You lost your mind to palm wine long ago.'

Loco laughed. 'That mind I lost to palm wine, I call it back and it is saying Sabi our friend is where you and I will both be when we can no longer be seen at this beer parlour,' he went on with more gaiety in his voice. 'Make no mistake about it; Madam See-Well will not miss you. She will only miss your money.'

'I am under no illusion on that,' Paik said. 'The only thing Madam See-Well sees well is money. I tell you that woman is in competition with the churches for money as for crowds. Look at the sea of people around you and imagine how much money she has squeezed out of them. I tell you this woman is going to hell through the popular path – the love of money.'

'You should have added: as we are going to the gnashing place through another popular path – drunkenness.'

'Loco, you can always be relied on to jab yourself.'

'Yeah,' Loco groaned, smiling wryly. 'Madam See-Well is in competition with the churches. She is the wicked one that went to plant weeds among the wheat. And these weeds are truly making people insane.'

'But the wicked one planted the weeds at night when the farmer who planted the wheat was asleep. The pastors are not asleep; they are awake. Even now you can hear them howling over there. How then is Madam See-Well able to plant her weeds among the wheat?'

'Yes, the pastors are awake; but they are only awake in money, not in spirit. In spirit, they are not merely asleep, they are dead. The pastor howling in the direction you were pointing, is he a man of God howling the spirit? No. He is a hyena and a wolf howling for meat.'

'Well, I am no sheep for him,' Paik spat

'Neither are all the foxes here,' Loco smirked, shaking his head, vigorously.

'The guys in the churches look at the sky and see houses; I look at the sky and see nothing. 'They are out there howling for the houses they see while I am here soaking myself to escape the emptiness I see,' Paik said belching.

'You keep vomiting gas leaving the real thing down there,' Loco spat. 'The air is not hungry. It does not need the gas from your belly. It is the ground and the ancestors down there that are thirsty. Spill something from your intestines to them.'

Paik laughed.

'Yeah, everyone is dancing the dance of his hope or his lack of hope,' Loco said.

'I don't understand.'

'Unless you drink to my level, you can't understand me. At the level of drunkenness I am now, only spirits understand me.'

Paik laughed.

'The drunk has no one but liquor. So as he walked alone home, he needs alcohol to talk to,' Loco said.

'You are right, though I would have loved you to be wrong,' Paik said.

For a while no one spoke.

'I am more at home here than in the church,' Paik said, breaking the silence.

'With your heart in the bottle, how can it be in the chalice also?' Loco said.

For a while neither of the two drunks spoke.

'Look at this mammoth crowd, and they say there is no money in the country,' Loco said breaking the silence. 'What are all these people paying Madam See-Well with?' he asked rhetorically.

'I wonder.'

'Sabi, my dear friend,' Loco groaned. 'Such a good man lost to death with his boots on.'

'Hmmm ...,' Paik grunted.

'He was such a good man with a good heart,' Loco said. 'I think God should look at his heart and not his liver.'

Paik laughed. 'You are crazy Loco,' he said, standing up to go relieve his bladders that were bursting with urine.

'Paik, beer and palm wine have kicked you out of shape,' Loco said laughing. 'You have twisted out only to twist in again.'

'If liquor has kicked me out of shape, it has left its signatures on your face; yes, it has spotted your face with chameleon faeces as the badge of what you did on earth and the powder Madam See-Well smeared your face with,' Paik said, laughing.

'On earth, Sabi was a walking keg of palm wine,' Loco said. 'In hell, he will be a bar of sorts to the demons in hell.'

Again, Paik laughed.

'Sabi really soaked himself when he was around,' Loco said with a mischievous gleam on his face. 'If anyone should know, I should. He had no friend like me. In hell, I believe the palm wine in his body should be able to quench the fire in hell.'

'You have said something there,' Paik said, taking a sip at his beer. 'I am sure a palm tree will sprout out of Loco and he will climb it out of hell.'

'You have also said something there,' Loco said, laughing.

'Hell, I wonder what kind of place it is,' Paik said.

'Don't worry; you won't wonder long since you will soon be there,' Loco said.

'Mmmm ...,' Paik drooled.

'Why should you wonder when the Bible has told you what it is?' Loco went on. 'It is a place of torment and gnashing of teeth, not a place for belching and long hiccups.'

'I wonder if hell is near heaven,' Paik said as if he had not heard what Loco said.

'Why do you keep wondering about things the Bible has settled?' Loco said. 'What kind of Thomas are you turning out to be? Hell is next door to heaven. The Bible says so or have you in your drunkenness forgotten the story of Lazarus and the rich man?'

'I am just wondering so many things in my rambling head,' Paik said.

'Like you, I am also wondering so many things,' Loco said. 'I know Sabi's father will make heaven. I am not wondering this one. But I wonder if the father will hear the cry of the son in hell the way Lazarus heard the cry of the rich man in hell and do nothing,' Loco said more to himself than to Paik.

'You are surely saying something weighty there,' Paik said 'I am getting to lintel level,' he went on, belching.

Loco laughed. 'We should be on our way then,' he said turning about on his seat. 'I don't have the strength to carry two bodies home. I don't even have the strength to carry my legs with me; of course, I have the strength to carry my stomach with all that is in it.'

Chapter Ten

On earth, Bilba was a resourceful man as he was a man of faith. When confronted by problems he had a way of getting round them. He was a demon adept at resolving knotty and tricky problems.

Before he got married, a girlfriend had clung to him like a bee to honey. She would not let him go when he wanted to. He liked the girl, but she seemed full of bad luck so much that some people called her a hoodoo and bad market. Unlike the girl, he was a sonsy whose friends called him good market. When the girl would not leave him, he told her he was seeking the face of God and wanted to be left alone.

His father died leaving a farmland for him and his elder brother as inheritance. Custom did not provide who between a younger and elder brother would share land left for the two as inheritance. However, with regard to chattels, custom provided it was the younger person that always shared things.

Bilba knew his elder brother to be a very greedy man who if allowed to share the land would cheat him. So, he made a case before the elders of the clan he and his elder brother invited for him to be the one to share the land left for them.

'If a group of drunks buy a keg of palm wine, it is the youngest person among those who bought the wine that shares the liquor,' Bilba said to the elders. The custom he cited was well known to everyone and from the way the elders were nodding their heads, it was clear what he said struck a chord in them.

'But you are a fervent Christian who sees nothing good in liquor,' the elder brother remonstrated.

'Liquor and the practice of sharing it are two different things,' Bilba countered. 'Liquor is no doubt unholy, but the choice by custom of who shares it is holy. Liquor may be insane, but the choice of who shares it is sane.'

'So, something clean can come from something unclean?' the elder brother interposed with a tinge of anger.

'Outside sharing things,' Bilba continued, ignoring what his elder brother had said; 'if a senior and younger brother are eating food together, the senior is required to leave some of the food for the younger brother and not finish the whole food with him.'

This custom was also well known by everyone. The elders, by the expressions on their faces, also seemed to like what he had said.

'What is the bearing of what you are saying on what we are here for?' his elder brother asked, heatedly. 'We are talking of sharing land and you are talking of an elder brother leaving food for his younger brother; do you want me to leave the whole land for you?'

'Not by any means,' Bilba said. 'What I am saying is that custom confers dignity on an elder brother that either prevents him from condescending to do certain things or disentitles him to certain benefits that would take something from his dignity. Sharing things is not a dignifying thing; neither is eating food to the last morsel with one's younger brother dignifying.'

'So, you are here to save me from embarrassing my dignity?' the elder brother asked with undisguised scorn on his face.

'If that is the interpretation you give what I am saying, you are right,' Bilba said. 'Again, while a younger brother can inherit the widow of his elder brother, the elder brother cannot inherit the widow of his younger brother,' he went on in a tone his elder brother found stinging.

'I can't believe what I am hearing,' the elder brother said full of angst. 'You even wish me dead so that you can inherit my wife?'

'You know I don't wish you dead and can't wish you dead,' Bilba said. 'I am only making a case before the elders why by custom I should be the one to share the land our father left for us.'

The elders decided the case in favour of Bilba and he shared the land equally between him and his elder brother. Though he shared the land equally between the two, his elder brother was not happy, an indication he would have done differently had he shared.

Bilba had two dogs. One was a glutton and impatient. Whenever, he was eating food, the gluttonous and impatient dog would stand in front of him as if to seize the food from him. Instead of kicking the dog or otherwise chasing it away as others did, he would midway into eating the food go to the other dog lying far away from him and put out some of the food to it. The gluttonous and greedy dog finding in the long run that going to stand by him while he ate was not paying it, took to lying beside the other dog to await his pleasure.

Freeing his son from hell required resourcefulness. Would he be able to mobilize such resourcefulness and unleash on this task?

Chapter Eleven

Heaven was flooded with light. Light crawling, light spanning, light creaming, light spotting, light shimmering, light blinking, light chiming, light spitting, light flaring, light streaming, light doting, light shadowing. The effervescent throw and spiral flow of light through the space making up heaven was so dazzling, magical and bewitching as to cast spells and possess souls.

In the midst of the mass of light in heaven sat His Peace. The light was with His Peace and the light was His Peace. There was no His Peace without the light and there was no the light without His Peace. The source of all light in heaven was peace. Without peace there would have been no light in heaven and without light there would have been no His Peace.

Hell was flooded with fire. Fire thickening, fire grooving, fire banding, fire sheeting, fire crimsoning, fire flaring, fire everywhere. As the case was with heaven, it was with hell. In the midst of the fire in hell sat His Havoc as the devil was popularly called in hell. There was no His

Havoc without the fire and no fire without His Havoc. Turmoil was the cause of fire in hell. Without turmoil, there would have been no fire in hell.

Walking into heaven was not just walking into the presence of His Peace but walking into His Peace and his throne. It was an awesome and taking experience that overthrew the mind and numbed the limbs.

Heaven was not only a place of enchanting lights, it was a song of holy and spiritual presence. It was a song of love, peace and unity. Heaven was not only a place of shimmering and chiming lights, it was a dance of peace and happiness.

When Bilba first walked into heaven, he felt an electrifying surge of peace and happiness flapping through him like the wings of a bird in flight. But the joy and peace of heaven soon fizzled out when he heard the plaintive cry of his son in hell. Now sitting in heaven, sadness and anger were also sitting in his heart like the sworn chiefs of Abaye.* Both joy and peace had forsaken

---

* The sworn chiefs of Abaye were chiefs who swore never to smile while poverty feasted on the people of the town who had nothing to feast on. After their death, grave-looking statues were erected for them in the ancient town of Abaye. These statues still standing in the ancient town are popularly referred to as the sworn chiefs of Abaye.

him. Heaven formerly adorned in the majestic raiment and apparels of a king was now wearing the rags of a beggar that was an eyesore. Now and then this beggar limped forward and extended a threadbare hand to him for alms.

Bilba did not know that the source of the light in heaven was peace. Neither did he know the cause of fire in hell was turmoil. As he did not know these secrets of heaven and hell, no heavener or heller knew.

For days, Bilba thought of how to quench fire in hell to relieve his son or how to import it into heaven for heaveners to taste what his son was going through, but found no way. Living close to angels, it seemed the resourceful demon in him that solved knotty problems has fled him. Am I becoming an ass in mind? Am I becoming Jahut the assy man of Kabak? he wondered despairingly.

As a child, his father had told him the story of Jahut who thought little because he had no brains. On a small solitary country path, Jahut was driving his ass home. Straddling the ass were two heavy sacks of soil Jahut was taking home from his farm to plaster his hut. From the tottering manner the ass was walking and the way it was groaning, it was clear the load it was carrying was too heavy for it. What was apparent to an onlooker did not seem apparent to Jahut. In his hand was a stick he was using to whip the ass to make it move faster despite the crushing load on its back.

The path Jahut and his ass were walking on was delivering Jahut and his ass to Kabak a village of about forty or so houses. Tall trees like sentinels were scattered round the village as if to secure it from the forest that might rush upon it and swallow it up. Indeed, myth had it that once upon a time, the forest had actually swallowed the village. The village was only vomited by the forest when a medicine man beseeched the forest.

In Kabak, the wind and the sky talked to the villagers. Some villagers heard the wind and the sky and did what the twosome bid them do. Others neither heard the wind nor the sky and so could not do the bidding of the duo. Jahut was one of the people who could not hear the wind or the sky and so could not do what the twosome were telling him until it was too late. For weeks, the wind and sky had been telling everyone that rain was imminent. The clouds in the sky told the people this. The heat in the air and the wind direction also told them this. Everyone heard the wind and the sky early except Jahut who only saw what the pair had been telling everyone was coming.

Kabak was a threadbare countryside. It was made threadbare by wind and rain erosion. In Kabak, arable soil for farming was also what was used to plaster houses. This soil was hard to come by. Because the soil was hard to find, people took to the forest and the bushes early to scrape the soil they would use to plaster their huts. Not Jahut who took no thought. He only repaired to the forest when there was no soil to scrape to plaster his huts. Where he could have gotten soil to plaster his house, he could no longer do so because the soil there had already been excavated by other people. So, he had to go to his farm to get the soil. At a time other people were about going to their farms to cultivate them to plant crops, Jahut was taking his own farm home to plaster his house.

The ass has stopped walking. Jahut has stopped walking too. He was flogging the ass to move on and grunting *hassurr hassurr* - assy phrases, to move the ass on, but the ass did not move. It wanted to rest the assy way – with load on its back. A better way to rest would have been hastening home to get the load off its back or lying down on its side with the load on the ground on its way home. But this is not the assy way of resting. The assy way of resting is to stand on one spot with heavy load on the back.

Jahut continued to flog the ass howling *hassurr hassurr.* He could not think of another way of getting the ass moving again or taking the load off it for it to rest.

As Jahut flogged the ass, Lamet came by. Lamet was a village school teacher seen in the village as a walking and talking book. He rarely talked to people. But he talked a lot to himself while walking or sitting. When he came by Jahut and his ass, he stopped and regarded the scene with a sagely bearing, shook his head and moved on talking to himself. 'The world is sick. I will like to write a book that will heal the world. I will like to write a book with medicinal properties that will heal any sick man who reads it. I will like to write a purgatory book that purges the reader of his sickness and admits him into the heaven of health. Look at the assy condition of the world, just look at it! Look at the assy condition of the man behind me and that of his ass. Are these not enough to make one sick? Why can't the man take some of the load off the ass? Why did he stay this long before going to fetch soil to plaster his house? Between him and the ass who should be flogged? Why was the ass standing with load on its back instead of lying down on its side? Why is stupidity growing beards and going grey without a leash on it? An assy, ashen and dusty fate surely awaits the world.

Am I becoming Jahut the assy man of Kabak? Bilba wondered again, despondently. Am I?

Chapter Twelve

While Bilba was still trying to find a way of putting an end to hell or heaven, the devil suddenly appeared in heaven to the shock of His Peace and everyone. Carrying with him a long line of demons, the devil appeared in heaven towards evening. He was indeed a very fearsome sight. The flurry and sudden way he appeared for a while created panic and confusion in heaven.

This was the first time the devil was appearing in heaven since he became the fallen angel. His Peace and his angels appeared as shocked and terrified as other denizens of heaven. What was the meaning of this, everyone in heaven was wondering. While heaveners were yet to recover from their shock and confusion caused by his appearance, the devil spoke, 'those of you with relations in hell can now appreciate that I am not as bad as you were made to believe while on earth,' he said drawing in a deep breath. 'You have pleaded for reprieve for your loved ones in hell, how much good have your pleas secured for your loved ones? If I were the one showing this lack of compassion, you will say it is the way of the Wicked One. Now that it is not me, it is murmurs and whispers I am hearing not swearing and curses. What did your loved ones do to burn in fire for eternity? What did I do to be in the fire I have been from the beginning of time? All I did was to nudge the hand of Eve to pluck a fruit she and Adam had been stretching their hands towards since they were created. All I did was to whet their appetite for the fruit of a tree His Peace himself created and placed before them, a fruit they had all along wanted to eat but His Peace had forbidden them from eating. For merely whetting Eve's appetite and nudging her hand, I was sentenced to hell for eternity. Now, how fair is this? How proportionate is my punishment to my offence? You sent your child to deliver a message. The child delivers a wrong message and you cut his tongue; how proportionate is the punishment you mete out to the offence the child committed?'

For a while, no one spoke. But if no one spoke, many people were agitated and restive. Heaven was seized by waves of resentment and anger. Soon grumblings and hissing grew out of resentment and anger, and protest and recrimination grew out of grumblings and hissing.

'Sending people to hell is rough justice,' someone said in a voice full of bitterness.

'Jersey justice is what one sees with His Peace,' another person cried. 'A hundred lashes for stealing a pin.'

'Punishment comes in tons here while rewards come in pints,' said another person.

'Here punishment pours while rewards trickle.'

'His Peace should know that rough justice is injustice.'

'He should know that justice is the foundation of peace.'

'Without justice there can be no peace.'

Because heaveners did not know without peace there could be no heaven, they could not say so. While they were talking, the devil and his demons disappeared the way they came. The disappearance of the devil and his demons was so sudden that it generated about the same panic their appearance had.

When panic lifted, goo took over. Goo was everywhere, on faces, in voices and even on the floor of heaven.

'The cursed one,' an angel full of goo said after the devil and his demons had left.

'The cursed one?' a heavener wondered aloud.

'The cursed one,' the angel repeated. 'He cursed your loved ones with hell while His Peace blessed you with heaven.'

'For me, there is no heaven without my son,' Bilba said. 'For me, heaven is worse than hell with my son out there wailing and gnashing his teeth.'

'He will always be an accuser,' an angel said looking like one in a trance.

'For good cause, you should add,' a heavener said.

'At least this time he only accused His Peace; he did not tell us to curse His Peace and die the way he did the other time,' said another heavener. '

Surprisingly His Peace said nothing all the while the devil was around and after his departure. Though he said nothing, he seemed to have lost a lot of peace during the entire episode. Losing peace, light in heaven dimmed.

Clouds always moved across heaven writhing like earthworms on dust. Since he arrived heaven, Bilba liked watching the clouds moving across the sky especially when he was in the solitude of the wilderness of heaven. Now his eyes were in the sky watching clouds that were moving across the sky.

Chapter Thirteen

A few days after the devil made his shocking appearance in heaven, Bilba and Konsa sneaked out of heaven. Moving in the direction of hell, the two souls came by a demon that had also sneaked out of hell and was heading towards heaven.

'Kind souls, where are you going?' the demon asked the two men.

'We are going to hell,' Bilba said.

'To hell?' the demon asked, shock branded on his face like an ugly tatoo. 'What gonzo is taking you to hell?'

'To see our relation there,' Konsa said.

'This is strange,' the demon said looking even more shocked than before. 'I have never had a tale like yours before.'

'You are now hearing it,' Bilba said.

'Going to hell every damned soul wants to flee from; what a weird trip? Do you want to be damned?'

'We are already damned,' Bilba said.

'Seriously, are you going to hell?'

'Seriously we are going to hell.'

'What for?'

'To rescue a loved one.'

'You will not be able to rescue your loved one. Instead, you will find yourselves in the pit of hell; who will rescue you?'

'No problem, we will remain in hell with him,' Konsa said.

'Are you out of your minds? Do you know how terrible hell is?'

'We know.'

'No, you don't. You only think you do, but don't in actuality. Hell is indeed hell. Hell is living through the anger of His Peace which is a consuming fire.'

'Well, perhaps we don't know hell,' Bilba said. 'Can you help us achieve our mission? Can you help two lame dogs over a stile?'

'Remember I am a demon; have you ever heard a demon assisting anyone achieve anything except perhaps a fell goal? What demons do is to get people into damnation, not out of it,' the demon said.

'Yes, rain may beat the leopard, but it does not wash away its spots,' Bilba said going to sit by a boulder on the side of the road. 'Yes, character is set in stone. A tortoise will always be a tortoise; it can never be a dove.'

'Yes, the tortoise will always carry his tribal marks wherever he goes,' Konsa said going to sit with Bilba on the boulder. 'It's vain going to the swine for soap.'

Unknown to Bilba and Konsa, the stone they were sitting on was the border stone between heaven and hell. It was the embankment or fence that kept hell away from heaven. But for it, hell would flow into heaven. If the boulder was rolled away, peace will forsake heaven and hell would overrun it.

Like Bilba and Konsa, no one in heaven or hell knew this huge stone was the fence between heaven and hell. Neither angels nor the devil and his demons knew the stone was the hedge between heaven and hell. Only His Peace was privy to this secret.

Apart from being a wall between heaven and hell, the boulder had under it the secrets of heaven and hell. No one ever sat on the huge stone without one of the secrets of heaven and hell under it appearing in the sky or something strange happening to he who sat on it. Sitting on the big rock was like pulling a trigger to release a secret of heaven or hell.

While sitting on the boulder thinking of how to rescue his son from hell as he had always thought, Bilba looked up and saw clouds writhing in the sky above him. He focused his gaze more intensely at what he thought were writings in the sky, and it turned out he was not seeing things. There were writings on clouds in the sky. Written in an imperfect form were the words *pite pote eisini detete linini.* These words meant nothing to Bilba because they were not words of a language he knew. He beckoned Konsa to come and see what he was seeing. Konsa was soon beside him also gazing at the writing in the sky. Like Bilba , the words in the sky meant nothing to Konsa because he did not know the language the words were from.

'What could these words possibly mean?' Bilba wondered aloud.

'They don't sound earthly to me,' Konsa said, mystified by the words.

'We are not on earth,' Bilba reminded him.

'Fine, they don't sound halleluiah to me,' Konsa said, smiling. 'You know they said halleluiah is our heavenly language.'

Bilba chuckled. It was the first time Konsa had heard him laugh since he arrived heaven.

'Something deep inside me tells me these words are a code to some secret,' Bilba said. 'I will search discreetly for their meaning. Who knows, they may hold the key to our agony in heaven?'

'Who knows?' Konsa intoned. 'When somebody should know, always nobody knows.'

Chapter Fourteen

Before Bilba's eyes left the sky, he committed to memory the cryptic words written on the clouds. Sitting or walking alone in heaven, he recited the words to himself in the hope that doing so would magically conjure intelligence in him that would unravel the meaning of the words. But no such magic happened.

What wand or talisman was he to wave before these words for them to open up and deliver their meaning to him? What magic carpet would fly him into their meaning? he kept wondering.

'Poor me, I left my brains on earth,' Bilba mourned. 'On earth, with my wits about me I would have cracked these words and taken out their meaning the way I will crack palm kernel. Poor me, I have gone assy and ashen in heaven. Though I have embraced the tree of knowledge and wisdom here, I don't seem to have regain all my knowledge and wisdom. Poor me.'

Because he felt the words held a big secret, Bilba was initially reluctant inquiring of their meaning from anyone. He wanted to find out their meaning by his own mental exertion. However, when his mental exertion of reciting the words to himself could not conjure their meaning as he had hoped, he began asking heaveners discreetly about the meaning of the words. In doing so, he would not recite the whole expression, but only one or two words of it.

'*Pite pote,*' I have never heard such eerie words before,' said the first heavener he asked the meaning of the words. 'Where did you hear these words?' he asked.

Bilba was pissed. How would where he heard the words help the intelligence of the man to know the meaning of the words? he thought angrily. He had no intention telling anyone where he read the expression. 'Don't bother where I heard the words,' he said to the man. 'Knowing where I heard them would not help you know their meaning if it could not help me.'

The second heavener he asked the meaning of *linini* said the word sounded cultic to him. He had never heard such word before. Where did Bilba hear it?

'Human beings,' Bilba muttered. 'They are all the same – crap. No intelligence; only irritating questions. Someone was asked if it is true people from his village answer questions with questions; he asked, "who told you?"

The third heavener Bilba asked the meaning of *eisini detete* said the words were esoteric words he thought must be from spirits of the air.

Esoteric words from spirits of the air? Bilba repeated to himself, his heart beating fast. The clouds he saw the writing on were in the air. Could spirits of the air have made the writing? If they did, what do they mean? Like before, he thought where he saw the words he was asking their meaning would not help his effort of finding their meaning. It may even compound or complicate the effort. Initially, he had a gut-feeling the words were made by His Peace. Now with this wild speculation that the words could be from spirits of the air, he was being drawn away from the direction his mind had been moving by perhaps a red herring that was sending him on a wild goose chase.

For days, Bilba inquired tactfully in heaven if anyone knew the meaning of the words *pite pote eisini detete linini* standing alone or in the combination they were composed, but found no one who even vaguely had heard of words sounding so eerie and cultic. When he was about giving up on his inquiry, he had a break from an unlikely quarter.

In one of his visits to the wilderness of heaven, Bilba dozed off while thinking of the expression *pite pote eisini detete linini* and John the Baptist. While asleep, John the Baptist appeared to him saying: *pite pote eisini detete linini* means if you boo and jeer at His Peace loudly, peace would forsake heaven; the boulder you sat on which released these words into the sky would roll off, bound through heaven and fall into hell setting off hell which will overrun heaven. Boos and jeers are to heaven what thunder is to a tree. Praise and adoration generate the peace of His Peace. Boos and jeers wither the peace of His Peace the same way the wind withers dry leaves on a tree.

Bilba was excited on hearing this. His excitement must have woken him for he woke up soon after. Though he knew what he was told was in a dream, this fact did not in any way temper his excitement on waking up. John the Baptist had once appeared to him and he seemed to him a bitter man. Though it did not seem to him at the time John the Baptist was letting him into the secret of the Tree of Knowledge that he was doing so out of bitterness he nursed against His Peace, but thinking of the situation later, it seemed so to him. If he was bitter, why was he bitter? It was not difficult for Bilba to see why. The man in leaves and animal skins if not sitting next to His Peace in heaven, should at least sit second to him. Yet he was nowhere near any of these. Anyone will feel betrayed by this and be bitter. If he was bitter, has his bitterness grown so thick to make him appear to him in his dream and tell him what he told him? Was he so consumed by bitterness to seek the destruction of heaven and His Peace? But if the wandering one wanted heaven destroyed, why couldn't he do it himself instead of relying on a *Johnny Just Come* like him? Well, it could be he was just forming the intent and recruiting those to help him carry it out. Perhaps knowing he had always loved and revered him more than any other prophet and seeing him sorrowing for his son, wanted to help end his anguish. Was the man in animal skins mad? the thought suddenly dropped into his mind. Was it madness that made him wear leaves and animal skins? Was it madness that made him talk to him the way he did? There was a song about the devil and John the Baptist by the heathens of Arbata:

> *The devil is not only a wanderer*
> *He is the ancient wanderer*
> *Wandering the wildernesses of the*
> *earth.*
> *The forest and the desert*
> *Are the wildernesses of the earth*
> *The devil wanders.*
> *Wilderness is from wild*
> *Wild is home to madness*
> *Wild is mad*
> *And so the forest and the desert*
> *Home to wild things*
> *Is home to mad things*
> *Home to wild happenings*
> *Is home to mad happenings.*
> *Whoever wanders the forest or desert*
> *Will most likely meet the ancient*
> *wanderer*
> *Wandering these untamed regions.*
> *Such a person may be smitten*

No, the man feeding on locusts and wild honey was not mad. He only wanted to help him and perhaps hit back.

John the Baptist had always been a man with the secrets of heaven. Bilba was sure what he told him in the dream was the biggest secret of heaven in the know of this man. As a man who knew secrets, maybe he had seen the secret in his heart and wanted to help him. The secret in his heart was to end heaven if his son could not be released from hell. But could the wandering prophet so resent His Peace as to want to destroy heaven knowing doing so would also destroy him? Well, people have been known to cut their noses to spite their faces. The man in leaves and skins had less stakes in heaven. It was those with more stakes that would lose more if heaven was destroyed. As for the man used to living on locusts and honey, he could easily cope in the wilderness. Wait, wait, wait. In all probability, John the Baptist had already taken to the wilderness of heaven as he took to the wilderness of the earth. Was it not in the wilderness of heaven he first appeared to him?

But John the Baptist was a humble man. He was not an arrogant man whose haughty spirit would sulk and seek to hit back when he was ignored. Oh no, humility did not come into it. He had long found out that humble people crave for regard no less than arrogant people. Humility is always courtesy to others, not low esteem for oneself.

Why were people always seeing things in the wilderness? It was in the wilderness Moses saw the burning bush. It was in the wilderness John the Baptist first appeared to him. It was in the wilderness he saw writings in the sky. From what John the Baptist had told him, this could turn out the burning bush that would rescue his son from hell. Was that not what Moses' burning bush accomplished for the Israelites in the hell of Egypt?

Chapter Fifteen

Konsa was the only one in heaven Bilba related his dream to. Konsa was more excited than Bilba when he narrated the dream to him. Konsa was an adventurous man who always got tremendous kicks from risky enterprises. He so much loved adventure that he undertook it even if it carried the risk of claiming his life. Though it was adventure that killed him on earth, in heaven he did not show less love for it on that score.

'While you may still be wondering if your dream holds any truth in reality, I have no doubt what you saw and heard was not a dream, but reality perhaps shy to appear to you while you are awake,' he said, excitedly. 'You did a lot for John the Baptist on earth; I am not surprised in heaven he is coming round to do much for you. You are reaping where you sowed.'

For days, Bilba and Konsa thought of how to recruit heaveners for the boos and jeers that would unleash mayhem on heaven without turning up a sound way. When they were about submitting to frustration, they found a way. Bilba felt contempt for himself for not thinking of the way they found much earlier. 'I am indeed assy in heaven,' he lamented.

The way Bilba found was recruiting people like him with crows to pluck with His Peace for them to boo and jeer at His Peace. In recruiting rebels, he would not tell them the whole truth of what John the Baptist told him. He would tell them their boos and jeers would only wreck heaven for a while by importing a little hell into it. If His Peace has a taste of hell, he would reconsider his stance on everlasting hell. If he put the matter this way, those of them who so much relish heaven would go along with the plot. Slanting the truth a little in the direction of lies; was that not what the devil did to get Adam and Eve eat the forbidden fruit? Like he had always said, the last Lucifer was yet to arise. He bared his mind to Konsa.

'The idea sounds nice,' Konsa said. 'I believe everyone with relations in hell will go along with us.'

'I think the same way you do,' Bilba said. 'But we have to be discreet about it. Not only discreet, we have to be circumspect of who we lead into this plot even among those aggrieved by the torment their loved ones are going through in hell. There are faint-hearted heaveners with relations in hell who cannot muster courage to be part of what we want to do.'

'You are very right,' Konsa said. 'Some people would rather die in the fear of the repercussions of resisting oppression than rise up against it.'

As soon as they agreed on what to do, Bilba and Konsa in a surreptitious manner began recruiting people into their plot. They were surprised how many people they were able to recruit within a short time. When they had gotten the number they thought sufficient to accomplish the task, they moved to the way of accomplishing it.

At a meeting of the plotters, different views were mooted on the signal Bilba leading the rebellion should give for the rebels to boo at once. Some rebels said he should clap whenever there was silence in heaven.

'This is not a good signal,' one of the rebels said. 'Clapping suggests praising His Peace and that is not what we will be about.'

Many people agreed with the rebel that objected to clapping. It was too frequent an occurrence to trigger a rebellion.

'He should wave his hands then,' suggested another rebel.

'This also is not a good sign,' said another rebel. 'People are always waving their hands in heaven in praise of His Peace.'

Many people also agreed with the rebel that objected to waving of hands. Waving of hands like clapping of hands was too frequent an occurrence to be the signal for a rebellion. How were the rebels to know the waving hands were those of Bilba?

'He should whistle then,' said yet another rebel. 'Whistling is never in praise of His Peace. Instead it suggests something sinister. Like whispers, it suggests something ominous. Perhaps because whistles are unholy in heaven, since I have been here, I have never heard anyone whistle.'

'But we have been whistling past the graveyard here,' Bilba joked.

A couple of heaveners laughed at Bilba's joke

Many rebels agreed with the last suggestion. It was unanimously adopted by the plotters. At the agreed time, when there was silence in heaven, Bilba should whistle and boos and jeers would go off shattering peace in heaven and importing full hell as Bilba and Konsa believed; wreck heaven for a while by importing a little hell into it, as the other plotters thought.

On the appointed day, the rebels were all in heaven in the presence of His Peace. At the appointed time, a shrill whistle went off from Bilba like a canon shot in a silent night. The whistle was followed by deafening boos and jeers that took His Peace by surprise. Screaming in fright, the screams of His Peace and the sustained boos and jeers of the rebels rolled the boulder at the border between heaven and hell which whirled about before landing in hell with a loud, breaking sound. Fire and brimstone from hell scoured through the wilderness of heaven with the fury of an unchained lunatic consuming everything on its path. In no time, heaven was overrun by hell. Neither His Peace nor angels and other heaveners were seen in heaven again. They were all tossed into various black holes in dying stars. Bilba and Konsa were tossed into the same hole. As for hell, no one knows if it is still there or not. However, considering that God is not there to enforce it, it is likely that hell also expired with heaven.

It turned out that heaven walking like a cripple towards mankind fell many years ago without a word of this happening getting to the earth. So, the sons and daughters of Adam and Eve continued to wait on God and hope on heaven when both God and heaven have gone kaput.

'In the Garden of Eden, the tree of the knowledge of good and evil made Adam and Eve to sin,' Bilba said to Konsa in the black hole they were.

'In heaven it made us rebel against His Peace,' Konsa said.

'In the Garden of Eden, it changed man from being zombie to a knowing and thinking being.'

'In heaven, it has done the same thing.'

'If the tree of the knowledge of good and evil is frustrating God's plans like this, why did he create it?'

'I wonder. First, this tree frustrated his plan
to make heaven out of the Garden of Eden, only
for it to reappear in heaven to frustrate his plan to
give effect to his original plan of idyllic life.'
'The tree of the knowledge of good and evil
has turned out His Peace's albatross.'

Epilogue

A monstrous sight appeared in heaven – a dragon with nine tails and nine horns. The dragon was pregnant with fire and brimstone which he kept spitting out without the fire and brimstone in his belly finishing.

And a second and last war broke out of heaven and everyone was hurled out of heaven including God and all his angels. This war was caused not by the dragon or angel but by Bilba a human being that died and went to heaven. Those hurled out of heaven were not hurled out to the earth, but into black holes in dying stars.

And it came to pass that after the summer of heaven, fall came and went into winter without a spring. The Last Lucifer had arisen and arose where and when no one thought he would.